101 Dalmatians

This edition published by BRIMAR PUBLISHING INC. 338 Saint Antoine St. E., Montreal, Canada H2Y 1A3. Tel. (514) 954-1441. Fax (514) 954-1443. Produced by TWIN BOOKS, 15 Sherwood Place Greenwich, CT 06830 USA. Original concept: Brimar Publishing Inc. Page layout and design: CND International. Cover and box design: ZAPP. Image adaptation: Van Gool – Lefèvre – Loiseaux. © 1991 The Walt Disney Company.

It was a typical day at the Radcliff residence, with Roger working on his songwriting while Pongo stared out the window in boredom. On the street, a slender elegant Dalmatian was taking a walk with an attractive young woman. Pongo's heart missed a beat. And when he saw her pet carrying a book, he knew that the woman would be perfect for Roger.

Pongo ran for his leash, then barked at Roger to get his attention. It wasn't time for Pongo's walk yet, but Roger was so absent-minded that he didn't know the difference. "All right, boy, all right," said Roger. "We'll go to the park."

At the park, Pongo led Roger past the bench where the woman and her Dalmatian were sitting. Roger was so lost in thought that he didn't even notice them! Instead, he went to sit on the grass beside the pond. Pongo knew that he had to do something – fast.

Pongo grabbed Roger's hat off his head and brought it over to the bench where the woman was reading. She looked up from her book, but when Pongo turned to grin at Roger, she and the Dalmatian walked away.

Now that he had gotten so close, Pongo wasn't about to give up. When Roger snapped on his leash, Pongo pulled him down the path after the lovely pair. As soon as they caught up to them, Pongo wrapped the leash around the woman's legs. Then he wound it around her and Roger, forcing them together.

"I'm so sorry, miss!" cried Roger to the woman. "Please excuse me. I . . . I . . ."

"I must say!" she replied, trying to untangle herself.

While trying to free themselves, Roger and the woman tumbled into the pond. Pongo rescued the woman's hat and waited for Roger to begin scolding him. When Roger and the woman started to laugh, Pongo glanced over at the Dalmatian. She was smiling.

Soon afterward, Roger married Anita, and Pongo repeated the same vows to the beautiful Dalmatian, Perdita. The two happy couples moved into a cozy house by the park. One evening, an old

classmate of Anita's burst through the door, trailing cigarette smoke behind her. Nanny, the housekeeper, was extremely annoyed, especially since Perdita was expecting puppies. But Cruella De Vil ignored Nanny. "Let me know when the puppies arrive!" she instructed Anita before storming out of the house.

Although Cruella's visit had been unpleasant, everyone forgot about her as they bustled about, preparing for the day that Perdita would give birth. Finally, the big moment arrived. Pongo waited nervously in the hall with Roger.

Nanny announced the arrival of one puppy, then another and another. Altogether, fifteen puppies were born that night! With joy, Roger held up one of the newborns for everyone to see.

As Nanny and the Radcliffs congratulated the parents, thunder cracked outside. The door flew open, and Cruella swooped into the room, heading straight for the puppies. When she saw them, she cried, "Ugh! What horrid little white rats!"

Bristling, Nanny explained, "Dalmatians don't get their spots until later! Just wait and see."

Roger refused to sell the puppies at any price.

After Cruella stalked out, Roger told Anita, "Don't worry. That woman will never get her hands on our puppies."

Relieved, Pongo and Perdita devoted all their time to raising their family. Every day the puppies grew larger, and soon they began to develop their spots.

All of the puppies loved to watch television. Their favorite show was about a brave dog named Thunder. Whenever Thunder appeared on the screen, the puppies barked wildly.

One winter night, Roger and Anita took Pongo and Perdita out for their walk in the park. While they were gone, Nanny took the puppies into the kitchen and tucked them into their basket.

The doorbell rang, and Nanny hurried to answer it. On the porch stood a tall, skinny man and a short, fat one. "We're from the electricity company," said the skinny one, Jasper.

"But we didn't call for an inspection," answered Nanny.

Nanny tried to shut the door, but Jasper pushed against it and almost knocked her over. As Jasper ran upstairs, his brother Horace headed across the room. Nanny chased Jasper up the stairs.

When Nanny ran into the first room, Jasper slammed the door behind her. She yanked on the doorknob until the door flew open. Hurrying downstairs, Nanny discovered that the intruders had gone . . . and that they had taken the puppies with them.

The next morning, Cruella De Vil grinned when she read about the kidnapping in the newspaper. The phone rang, and she picked it up.

Roger suspected Cruella, and he told her so a few days later. But Anita didn't have the heart to believe Cruella would do such a thing.

Since everyone else was having trouble solving the crime, Pongo told Perdita, "It's up to us. We'll have to use the Twilight Bark to inform all the dogs in London."

That night, Pongo called out the message. A Great Dane and a Scottish terrier heard it first, and they passed it on to a dog who had been sleeping nearby.

Before daylight, every dog in London had heard about the missing Dalmatian puppies. Soon the Twilight Bark traveled all the way out to the country.

Towser the bloodhound and Lucy, a goose, hurried to the top of a hill to alert the farm animals. Towser's bark reached Captain the horse, who awakened his two friends: an old sheepdog named the Colonel and a cat named Sergeant Tibs. "That's funny," said Tibs. "Two nights ago, I heard barking at the old De Vil mansion."

"How strange!" exclaimed the Colonel. "I suppose we'd better investigate. Let's go, Tibs."

They trudged through snow to the gloomy mansion. While the Colonel waited at the gate, Sergeant Tibs sneaked inside. There he found a room filled with dozens of Dalmatian puppies. They were watching television with two tough-looking men.

Tibs quickly reported back to the Colonel, then returned to find Cruella yelling at Horace and Jasper. Tibs was shocked to learn that Cruella was planning to make dog-skin coats out of the puppies!

Horrified, Tibs heard Cruella tell the kidnappers: "I'm not paying you to watch television. I want the job done tonight!"

After Cruella left, Tibs crept through a hole in the wall and whispered to the puppies, "You'd better get out of here if you want to save your skins. Quick, follow me."

One by one, Sergeant Tibs helped the puppies through the hole in the wall, and they followed him under the staircase, shaking with fright.

Suddenly, the dark shadow of a kidnapper loomed over them.

In the meantime, Danny the Great Dane had alerted Pongo and Perdita to the puppies' location. The two Dalmatians had hurried to the mansion, and when they saw Jasper threatening the puppies, they crashed through the window. As Pongo and Perdita fought the kidnappers, Sergeant Tibs led the puppies to safety.

After a fierce battle, Perdita and Pongo escaped and hurried to meet up with the puppies at the Colonel's barn.

Soon after Pongo and Perdita arrived, they discovered that the kidnappers had followed them. While the Colonel guarded the door, the Dalmatians retreated out the back. It wasn't long before Jasper and Horace pushed past the sheepdog and entered the barn.

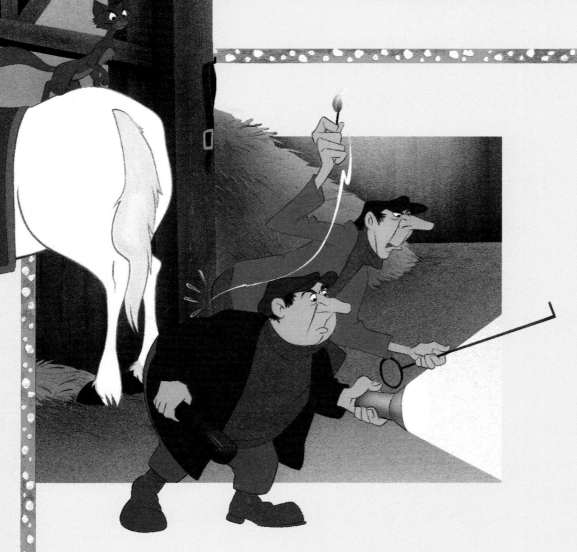

The two men poked at the hay and shone their flashlights in all the corners, but they found no sign of the puppies. They never noticed Tibs, who was perched on Captain's back. When the kidnappers paused behind the horse, Tibs whispered, "Ready, aim, fire!"

Captain's powerful hooves lashed out and kicked Jasper, then Horace, into the air.

The Colonel ducked as the two kidnappers flew over his head and landed outside in a snowbank. In the distance, Horace and Jasper could see the Dalmatians escaping. The kidnappers hurried back to their truck and took off.

In the snow, Pongo and Perdita did their best to keep the puppies moving. Although they were as tired and cold as the little ones, they encouraged the puppies not to give up. Pongo desperately hoped they would find safety before the kidnappers picked up their trail.

Pongo had just started to carry one of the puppies when a collie ran up to meet them. "We have shelter for you at the dairy barn across the road," the collie told Pongo. "You can rest, then get an early start in the morning."

"Thank goodness!" replied Pongo. "This way, everyone!" The dogs filed into the barn, where three gentle cows welcomed them.

"My, what a big family you have!" said Princess, one of the cows. "The poor little dears. They must be half-frozen."

When the cows learned that the puppies were starving, they offered them some warm milk. The puppies drank as much as they could, then settled down to sleep.

At dawn, the Dalmatians rose and set off again. As they crossed a road, they saw Cruella's car approaching. Pongo quickly hid the puppies in the woods.

After Cruella had passed, the Dalmatians emerged from the woods and found a Labrador who promised to help them.

The Labrador led the Dalmatians to a blacksmith's forge in a village. "You can catch a ride to London in a furniture van," said the Labrador, "but you'll have to hide until the engine's fixed."

As the dogs waited in the forge, Cruella and the kidnappers drove down the street. The dogs ducked beneath the window. When Pongo looked over at the puppies, he saw two of them playing in the soot.

"I have an idea!" Pongo cried. "If we all roll in the soot, we'll look like Labradors!" Soon all of the dogs had disguised their spotted coats with black soot.

In groups, the disguised puppies hurried toward the van.

When Cruella careered around the corner and saw so many dogs in one place, she became suspicious. She screeched to a stop just as a clump of snow slid off a roof and landed on one of the puppies.

When Pongo pulled the puppy out of the snow, his coat was washed clean. Every spot stood out against his white coat.

"Horace! Jasper!" shouted Cruella as Pongo shoved the last bunch of puppies into the van. The van took off, and Cruella followed in her roadster. Horace and Jasper jumped in their truck and headed down another road, hoping to cut off the van.

Cruella caught up first and bashed the van in the side, trying to force it off the road. The van driver shouted, "Hey! What in thunder are you trying to do?"

With a wild look in her eyes, Cruella rammed into the van again. Suddenly a one-lane bridge loomed before them.

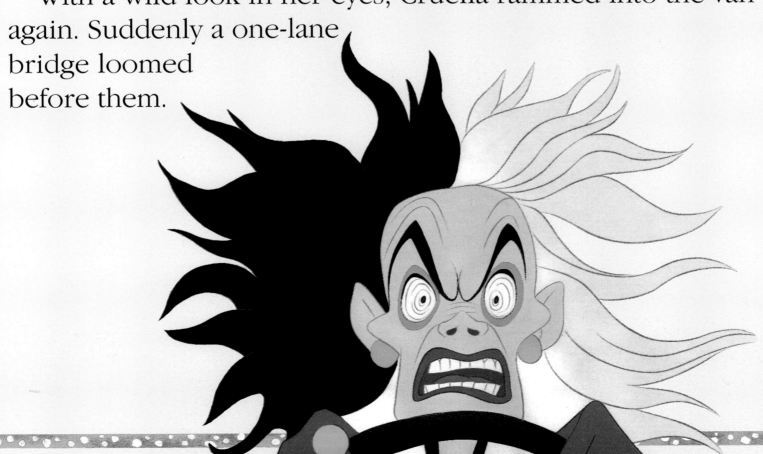

The van made is across
the bridge, but Cruella
plunged into a deep ravine.
The furniture van
continued on to London.
When it reached the Radcliff
residence, Pongo and the
others leaped
from the van.

They rushed into the house, and
Roger exclaimed, "Why, look at all
these Labradors!"

Nanny was the first to discover the
truth. "No, they're covered with soot!" she cried.

Anita and Nanny tried to wipe the soot off.
"They're all here, the little dears," said Nanny.
"And there's a whole lot more!"

When Nanny and the Radcliffs began counting, they
discovered that there were one hundred and one
Dalmatians!

Roger sat down at the piano
and began to play. 'I'll have to
write a song about our new
home," he said, smiling. "And
I'll call it 'Dalmatian
Plantation'!"